This Is a ~~Squirrel~~ (TACO!)

By Andrew Cangelose

Illustrated by Josh Shipley

ONI PRESS

This is a squirrel.

Hi, my name is Taco, 'cause my favorite food is tacos! I'm really excited to be in this book! I can't wait to help you learn all about squirrels like me!

Squirrels are some of the cleanest rodents in the wild. They are known for having silky, soft fur.

Squirrels love to eat nuts, acorns,
and even tree bark.

Squirrels can pack large amounts of food into their cheeks to transport back to their nests.

Squirrels can rotate their ankles completely backward. This allows them to climb in any direction.

Squirrels are great tree climbers
and love to jump from branch to branch.

Some squirrels, called flying squirrels, can glide through the air for distances of over 150 feet!

You've got the wrong squirrel!
My cousin Barry is the flyer
in the family!
AHHHHHHHHHH!!!!!!

Then they glide gently to the ground
for a graceful landing.

The hawk is the natural predator of squirrels, swooping down from the air to swipe them right off the ground.

Whoa! Time out! This book needs fewer hawks and way more tacos. And when I say fewer hawks, I mean ZERO!

The hawk is th   ator of squirrels, swoopi   he air to swipe th   und.

The hawk is the predator of squirrels, swooping through the air to swipe them right off the ground.

The ~~hawk~~ is the natural predator of squirrels, swooping do__ ___ ___ __ to swipe them right off

TACO

The ~~hawk~~ is the natural predator of

TACOS

~~squirrels,~~ swooping down from the air to

swipe them right off the ground.

Now that's more like it!

TACO

TACOS

The ~~hawk~~ is the natural predator of ~~squirrels,~~ swooping down from the air to swipe them right off the ground.

The ~~hawk~~ TACO is the natural predator of ~~squirrels~~ TACOS, swooping down from the air to swipe them right off the ground.

Taco, the squirrel

(and not an actual giant, talking taco),

is the natural predator
of <u>tacos</u>.

Squirrels are great eaters
and can eat their body weight in
tacos ~~food~~ in just a ~~week~~ day.

PUBLISHED BY
**Oni-Lion Forge
Publishing Group, LLC.**

WRITTEN BY
Andrew Cangelose

ILLUSTRATED & LETTERED BY
Josh Shipley

EDITED BY
**Shawna Gore &
Grace Scheipeter**

onipress.com
facebook.com/onipress
twitter.com/onipress
instagram.com/onipress

First Edition: July 2022
ISBN 978-1-63715-076-4

Library of Congress Control Number: 2017963044

Printed in China.

1 2 3 4 5 6 7 8 9 10